Citizen of New York

Banquet to Señor Matias Romero

Citizen of New York

Banquet to Señor Matias Romero

ISBN/EAN: 9783744784665

Printed in Europe, USA, Canada, Australia, Japan

Cover: Foto ©Andreas Hilbeck / pixelio.de

More available books at **www.hansebooks.com**

BANQUET

·

Señor Matias Romero,

Envoy Extraordinary and Minister Plenipotentiary
from Mexico to the United States,

BY THE

CITIZENS OF NEW YORK.

OCTOBER, 2nd, 1867,

New York, September 16, 1867.

His Excellency, Señor Matias Romero,

Envoy Extraordinary and Minister Plenipotentiary, from Mexico,

Washington, D. C.

Sir:

The undersigned citizens of New York, desirous to testify in some public manner their esteem for your character as the representative of the Mexican Government, their appreciation of the services which you have rendered your country by steadily adhering to its cause under the greatest discouragements, and their interest in the welfare of Mexico, invite you to a Dinner at such time as may suit your convenience to appoint.

Respectfully, your obedient Servants,

PETER COOPER,	WM. C. BRYANT,
WM. H. ASPINWALL,	JAMES W. BEEKMAN,
PAUL SPOFFORD,	HIRAM BARNEY,
M. H. GRINNELL,	WM. E. DODGE, JR.,
H. R. VAN DYCK,	JOHN JAY,
HENRY CLEWS,	HENRY WARD BEECHER,
SAM'L G. COURTNEY,	DAN'L BUTTERFIELD,
JAMES ROBB,	THEODORE ROOSEVELT,
CHAS. W. SANDFORD,	JOHN A. STEWART,
FRANCIS SKIDDY,	HENRY A. SMYTHE,
SHEPARD GANDY,	DAVID HOADLEY,
PARK GODWIN,	RUFUS INGALLS,
WM. R. GARRISON,	JAS. R. WHITING,
BENJ. HOLLIDAY,	J. GRANT WILSON,
ELLIOTT C. COWDIN,	WM. G. FARGO.

A

Washington, September 18, 1867.

GENTLEMEN :

I have been honored with the letter you had the kindness to address me on the 16th instant, inviting me to a Dinner at such time as may suit my convenience to appoint.

It is very gratifying to me, gentlemen, that such good friends of mine and prominent citizens of New York as you, who have encouraged me so much throughout the contest, would now tender me this significant demonstration, selecting a time when I am about returning home, after having obtained, thanks to a merciful Providence, the patriotism of the Mexican people and the noble sympathy of the people of the United States, a crowning success in all the objects of my labors.

I take this flattering demonstration to be the renewed expression of your sympathy for the efforts of the Mexican people in defending the Independence of their Country and the institutions of their choice, and for the patriotic conduct of the Republican Government which did so much to achieve success.

It will afford me a great deal of pleasure to meet you in the proposed social celebration of our success, which will, in my opinion, prove advantageous to this country as well as to my own, and for which we are so much indebted to you.

Availing myself of the privilege you have been good enough to grant me, I will name Wednesday, the 2d of October, as convenient to me, and hope that this time may also be acceptable to you.

I am, Gentlemen, with high respect, most truly,

Your obedient servant,

M. ROMERO.

To Messrs. William Cullen Bryant, Peter Cooper, William H. Aspinwall, Paul Spofford, James W. Beekman, Henry A Smythe, H. H. Van Dyck, Samuel G. Courtney, Benjamin Holliday, Rev. Henry Ward Beecher, James Robb, Maj. Gen'l Butterfield, William E. Dodge, Jr., Theodore Roosevelt, Maj. Gen'l Sandford, Francis Skiddy, Henry Clews, William R. Garrison, Park Godwin, David Hoadley, Wm. G. Fargo, Maj. Gen'l Ingalls, Shepard Gandy, John A. Stewart, Judge Whiting, J. Grant Wilson, Elliott C. Cowdin, John Jay, Moses H. Grinnell, Hiram Barney,
Of New York.

LETTERS.

DEPARTMENT OF STATE, Washington, Sept. 27, 1867.

To HIRAM BARNEY, JAMES W. BEEKMAN, WILLIAM E. DODGE, Jr., THEODORE
    ROOSEVELT, and HENRY CLEWS, Committee, &c., New York.

GENTLEMEN:

      I regret that business here will deprive me of the pleasure of
being present at the entertainment so justly and properly tendered by eminent
citizens of New York to my highly respected and esteemed friend, Mr. ROMERO,
the Minister who has so long represented the Republic of Mexico at this Capitol,
with distinguished ability, fidelity, frankness, and courtesy. With thanks for your
kind invitation, and with the assurance of high respect,

              I am, your obedient servant,

                     WILLIAM H. SEWARD.

        HEADQUARTERS ARMIES OF THE UNITED STATES,
           Washington, D. C., Sept. 27, 1867.

MY DEAR SIR:

      Your polite invitation for me to be present at a Dinner to be given
to Señor ROMERO, Mexican Minister, &c., is received. I regret to think it improb-
able that I will be able to leave this city at the time specified. I regret this because
of the high appreciation I have always held the recipient of your compliment in,
personally, and the sympathy I have felt for the cause which he has so ably and
zealously represented. His cause was our cause, to a greater extent probably than
will ever be appreciated, now that success has attended it. Failure would have
demonstrated how much we were interested in the success of the Liberals of our

Sister Republic. Hoping that you will have a pleasant time, and clearly demonstrate to Señor ROMERO the heartfelt sympathy of loyal Americans for the cause of free government in his country,

I subscribe myself,

Respectfully and truly, your friend,

U. S. GRANT, General.

HIRAM BARNEY, Esq., Chairman, &c.

Washington, September 30th, 1867.

GENTLEMEN:

I regret my inability to be present on the occasion of the complimentary Dinner which is to be given to Señor ROMERO, on the 2nd of October. Other duties detain me here. It would afford me great gratification to unite with you in complimenting one who has with eminent fidelity and ability represented the Republic of Mexico at Washington, during the trying period when his country and our own had difficulties of no ordinary character to surmount. From constant intercourse with him through those eventful years I can bear testimony to his unfaltering devotion to the cause of Constitutional freedom, and I am happy to congratulate him that he can, without molestation from foreign invaders, return to the Republic which he has so faithfully represented.

I am, very respectfully,

Your obedient servant,

GIDEON WELLES.

HON. HIRAM BARNEY, Chairman, &c.

DEPARTMENT OF STATE, Washington, 28th Sept. 1867.

GENTLEMEN :

Cordially sharing in your esteem for Mr. ROMERO, and in your appreciation of his character and eminent public services, it is with regret that I find that the pressure of official duties here will prevent my accepting your kind invitation to be present at the Dinner which has been tendered to him in New York.

With much respect, your obedient servant,

F. W. SEWARD.

HON. HIRAM BARNEY, Chairman, &c

U. S. Naval Academy, Annapolis, Md., Sept. 28, 1867.

Gentlemen :

I have the honor to acknowledge the receipt of your polite invitation to a Dinner given to Mr. Romero, Minister from our sister Republic of Mexico. I regret exceedingly that my public duties will prevent my being present on so interesting an occasion. I regret it the more as I have great respect for Mr. Romero, for the manner in which he has conducted the affairs of his Government in a time of severe trial, while residing near the United States Government, and I trust that he may receive from the citizens of his own country the kind attention he has received from the citizens of the United States.

Very respectfully and truly yours,

DAVID D. PORTER, Vice-Admiral.

Hon. Hiram Barney, Chairman, &c.

Pennsylvania Executive Chamber, Harrisburg, Pa., Sept. 30, 1867.

My Dear Sir :

I have the honor to acknowledge your kind invitation to be present at the complimentary Dinner to be given to Señor Romero, Envoy Extraordinary and Minister Plenipotentiary from Mexico. I should be much pleased to accept, but my business engagements will not permit, and I request that you will extend to your colleagues on the committee my thanks for their courtesy, and to your distinguished guest my kindest wishes for his personal welfare and for the future peace and prosperity of the Republic he so long and ably has represented at Washington.

Very respectfully, your obedient servant,

JOHN W GEARY.

Hon. Hiram Barney, Chairman, &c.

St. Nicholas Hotel, New York, Oct. 2, 1867.

Gentlemen :

I regret exceedingly that my engagements compel me to leave for Ohio this afternoon, which will deny me the pleasure of joining you at Dinner this evening,

S

and of expressing, in person, the high respect I entertain for your distinguished guest. During some of the darkest days of Mexico in her recent struggle against her foreign invaders, it was my fortune to see much of Señor ROMERO, and it is but doing him justice to say, that he never failed to bear himself with the courage and dignity fitting the official representative of a brave people contending against a powerful enemy for their liberties. My sympathies were always with that oppressed people, and it is a gratifying memory to me, that I never lost an opportunity, while a member of the administration, to do all in my power to encourage the Republicans of Mexico in their contest. And now that the struggle is ended in the triumph of the Constitutional Government, I am most happy to join you in the warmest congratulations to Señor Romero on the noble victory, and on the restoration of Republican Government in Mexico. Accept my thanks for the invitation with which you have honored me.

I have the honor to be,

Very respectfully, yours, &c.,

W. DENNISON.

HON. HIRAM BARNEY, Chairman, &c.

————————

Boston, Sept. 30, 1867.

MY DEAR SIR :

If I could leave home at present, I would certainly have availed myself of the privilege afforded by the Committee of which you are a member, to meet Mr. ROMERO, in company with a large number of eminent gentlemen, at a Dinner to be given to-morrow evening in New York, in recognition of his official services as the representative of the Government of Mexico, and in friendly recognition, also, of the interest in the welfare, freedom, and upward progress of Mexico, entertained by the people of the United States. It is not in my power to withdraw myself from other engagements here, but I am grateful for the opportunity, in a single written word, to declare my respect for the person of Mr. ROMERO, and my best wishes for his health and happiness. I trust that our own Government, and people will not omit to embrace every just occasion to express, in all fit and becoming ways, the paternal regard due from an elder American Republic to a younger and suffering member of the great family of free nations, seeking to establish industry, law, order, liberty, and religion on the basis of permanent and liberal Republicanism. Without selfishness on our part, but in a spirit of entire devotion to principles and ideas, which we ought to desire that other nations may in their own way work out to results useful and honorable to themselves, we can always remember (and conduct as if we remembered) that the United States, as a Government and as a people, stand at the head, and are to be looked to by all the world to lead in the cause of Republicanism and well ordered liberty. We can do this in the interest of peace, as well as of freedom; in the interest of commerce and education, as well as of national independence and popular institutions. A great career, covering long years of usefulness and glory, awaits America. May it be directed by generous minds—just, faithful, intelligent, and broad.

I am, most respectfully,

Your friend and servant,

JOHN A. ANDREW.

Hon. Hiram Barney, Chairman, &c.

Utica, Sept. 28, 1867.

Gentlemen :

I have the pleasure to acknowledge your invitation to dine with Señor Romero on Wednesday next. An engagement in Court, calling me at the same time to a distant county, will deprive me of the pleasure I should have in meeting your distinguished guest and those who will entertain him. Nothing, however, shall deprive me of sympathy with the occasion, and with the sentiment it typifies. Having seen something of Señor Romero during the sad trials of his country and of our own, I know how deservedly your courtesy and hospitality will be bestowed. Displaying a faculty for affairs which would be noticeable in any man, he has exhibited an unfaltering faith in liberty and humanity, and a placid self-possession in great perplexities which, reflecting honor upon him, at the same time prove how a just cause sustains and strengthens those who believe. The battle of ideas, fought in Mexico and for Mexico, was our battle. The stranger and the invader there, like the ingrate and the conspirator here, struck for caste ; Mexico, like America, struck for man, and shares with America, upon a common continent, the triumph of a common cause. You mean to bring around the same table, men separated by different latitudes, but cherishing purposes and hopes which mingle in spite of seas and climes. The thought is a timely one, and will serve as a pleasant greeting to the new Republic under the Southern Cross. I wish I might be one of those who will give in person to the departing Envoy their well-wishes for his country and himself.

With high esteem.

Your obedient servant,

ROSCOE CONKLING.

Hon. Hiram Barney, Chairman, &c.

———— ——— ———

Harrisburg, Penn., Sept. 30, 1867.

Hon. Hiram Barney, Chairman, &c.

I am in receipt of your invitation to participate in the complimentary Dinner to Señor Romero, on the 2d proximo, and sincerely regret my inability to be with you, on that interesting occasion, for I would be heartily glad to join with you in doing honor alike to your distinguished guest and the gallant people he represents, who like ourselves have so lately passed through the baptism of fire. Their cause was our cause, their enemies were our enemies, and therefore we rejoice at their victories almost as our own. Indeed it seems to me that the highest eulogy upon Señor Romero is embraced in the fact that he had so wisely discharged the duties of his high office as to have made it morally certain that if their victory had been longer delayed the banners of the two Republics would have waved over the same armies, and the sword of Sheridan would have been unsheathed in defense of the independence of Mexico. The services your guest was able to render to his country, by his wisdom, his patience, his devotion to her interests, and his unfailing faith in her ultimate triumph over all her enemies, will doubtless receive fitting recognition at the hands of his Government and his countrymen, but I cannot forbear repeating my regret that I am unable to be with you to bid Señor Romero good speed and a pleasant voyage on his return to the land he has served so faithfully and so well.

Sincerely yours,

SIMON CAMERON.

Nashville, Sept. 30th, 1867.

RESPECTED SIR:

I regret sincerely my inability to meet you and your worthy associates on this occasion. The time for the reässembling of Congress is not far off, and my previous engagements forbid my absence from this part of our country at present. It affords me great pleasure to be honored by such an invitation, and equally great to know that my fellow countrymen have done our country this honor by showing to the world that they have witnessed and appreciated the labor of one of the most earnest and devoted men and patriots of the age. Señor ROMERO understood from the begining the nature of the contest in which his country was engaged. He knew the character of the men who were struggling for her emancipation. He was inspired with a noble faith in the triumph of the principles of liberty, and the earnest character of its defenders. He never in the most gloomy period of his country's distress, wavered in his devotion to the cause, or abated his constant watchfulness and labors. He was no less the friend of our own Union than of his country's integrity, for he is the real friend of Republican Government. His faith in our own success was no less bright than it was in the final triumph of the Mexican Patriots. The present is a most honorable testimonial to an able, faithful, devoted patriot, to a true friend of the United States, and the cause of human liberty throughout the world. You have my sincere and earnest wishes for the complete success of the occasion, for the prosperity of all that feel a deep interest in your promised compliment, and especially for your honored and worthy guest.

Yours truly,

JOS. S. FOWLER.

HON. HIRAM BARNEY, Chairman, &c.

Natick, Mass., Sept. 28, 1867.

MY DEAR SIR:

I have to thank you for the honor of an invitation to the Dinner to be given by eminent citizens of New York to Señor ROMERO, Minister of the Republic of Mexico. It is, I assure you, a matter of regret that it is not in my power to unite in paying this compliment to a statesman who, during the troubled days of the wicked invasion of his country and the usurpation of its Government, was so steadfast in his devotion to independence and Republican institutions. I honor Señor ROMERO, not only for his fidelity to his own country in her great trials, but for his deep sympathy with our country in its struggle for existence. This tribute of respect, paid by so many honored citizens of the commercial capital of the Republic, will be an additional assurance to Señor ROMERO, that he will bear with him to his country the liveliest hopes of the people of the United States that the Republic of Mexico will now enter upon a career of progressive developement, under free institutions, where personal freedom will be protected by law and order.

Yours, ever,

HENRY WILSON.

HON. HIRAM BARNEY, Chairman, &c.

Detroit, Sept. 28, 1867.

DEAR SIR :

To-day's mail brings me your polite invitation to a Dinner in compliment to Señor ROMERO, the Minister of the Republic of Mexico to our Government. It would give me great pleasure to attend, but the shortness of the time and the length of the journey will deprive me of the pleasure. I cannot close, however, without testifying my high respect and even admiration for the character of Mr. ROMERO. Working his cause attentively during the terrible war, which tyrants and the tools of tyrants have waged in his afflicted country, to overthrow and extinguish popular rights. I have found him to be ever true and faithful to the great cause of Republican liberty. And even in the darkest hours he has manifested a constancy which disaster could not shake, and a faith in the ultimate triumph of his country's cause, at once touching and sublime. I am sure that JUAREZ, the distinguished statesman and patriot, under whom he has served so creditably near our Government, has not found a more trusty and efficient agent in promoting the true interests of Mexico; and it could only be a repetition of what is notorious, to say that in the management of the relations of his country with our own, he has secured himself, and justly, the reputation of a true and able minister. May his country be proud of him, and may she ever be served with equal wisdom, vigilance and energy.

Very truly and respectfully,

Your obedient servant,

J. M. HOWARD.

Hon. Hiram Barney, Chairman, &c.

Detroit, Sept. 28, 1867.

Dear Sir:

    I regret that engagements in Ohio will prevent the acceptance of the invitation of your Committee to be present at the complimentary Dinner given to Señor Romero, on the 2d of October. For Señor Romero, *personally*, I entertain the highest respect. During the darkest hours, when despotisms were combined with rebellions for the overthrow of Republican institutions upon this Continent, Señor Romero never faltered, doubted or wavered, hoping almost against hope. He stood alone, true to the Mexican Republic, true to the Government of the United States. How much this Government is indebted to the patriots of Mexico will never be known. They permitted no diversions upon our Southern borders by French bayonets, during our long and terrible struggle with rebellion. It is meet to do Señor Romero high honor, and again thanking you for the invitation, I regret my inability to be present.

Very truly yours,

T. CHANDLER.

Hon. Hiram Barney, Chairman, &c.

South Bend, Ind., Sept. 30, 1867.

My Dear Sir:

    I am glad to find by your letter that such a large number of the solid men of your city have united in a complimentary Dinner to Señor Romero, for so many years the Minister of the Mexican Republic at Washington, and whom I feel honored in being able to call my friend. Distance and other engagements prevent my attendance, but I send him, from my Western home, hearty congratulations that the heroic constancy of his people at last compels the whole world to call Mexico a Republic once more. Fortunate indeed was it for Mexico that in her hour of trial she had such a representative here. Denied recognition by the rest of the diplomatic corps, he never "bated jot of heart or hope" of the final triumph of his nation. Modest in his bearing, but firm in his position, always actively at work, explaining to all inquirers every phase of the struggle, correcting misstatements, and supplying the Administration and Congressmen with important information so often needed. Mexico seemed always in his heart and on his lips, and I rejoice with you and with him in its final triumph.

Yours, very truly,

SCHUYLER COLFAX.

Hon. Hiram Barney, Chairman, &c.

Lancaster, Sept. 28, 1867.

Gentlemen :

I have received your invitation to attend a Dinner to be given in compliment to Señor Romero, and being unable to answer in person, dictate the following :

I know of no occasion when it would afford me so much gratification to show my appreciation of the noble acts of an individual and of a nation. During the whole time that the United States have been carrying on an inter-partes war for existence, the distracted Republic of Mexico has been resisting the despotism of more than one foreign nation, independent of her own traitors. Having adopted an excellent constitution, she was fortunate enough to elect one of the ablest and most distinguished Presidents to administer it. He met every difficulty, and in defiance of every threat refused to surrender the interests of his country. I can think of but two men, Washington and William of Orange, who, under parallel circumstances, combined equally all the qualities of fortitude and patriotism. God gave him victory, and, as in their case, protected the cause of liberty. Posterity in Mexico will hardly realize the difficulties which this great man encountered. In this country that cause was most essentially promoted by the able and patriotic efforts of Señor ROMERO, without whose prudence and determination it would have been impossible to sustain the courage and confidence of his countrymen. The Republic of Mexico was very fortunate in the selection of her representative to this Government. Sagacious and cool, he managed his temper with admirable skill in the midst of most perplexing difficulties. With great delicacy he avoided all topics of controversy without sacrificing any of the rights of his country. This Government found no occasion to bestow any thing but honor upon her sister Republic. Whether during that whole war she did equal honor to herself, it does not become us, on this occasion, any more than Señor ROMERO, to inquire. It is to be hoped if we again become involved in similar difficulties with a foreign nation we may be both able and willing to maintain those principles which we deem it necessary for our national honor and safety to assert. I regret that the state of my health will make it impossible for me to be present at your Dinner,

And am, gentlemen,

Very faithfully yours,

THADDEUS STEVENS.

HON. HIRAM BARNEY, Chairman, &c.

Knoxville, Tenn., Sept. 30, 1867.

DEAR SIR :

It is with regret that I must forego the honor of being present at the complimentary Dinner tendered to Señor ROMERO, the diplomatic representative of the Mexican Republic. To his country as well as to ours, the last few years have been full of moment. There as well as here Republican government has been on trial, here by domestic treason, aided by foreign support, there by foreign enemies aided by domestic traitors. In both, signal success has rewarded the friends of free Republican government and done much to establish its principles in the estimation of mankind. Both have demonstrated that the most powerful, benign and magnanimous form of government is that which rests for support upon the will and the affections of the people. Both have incorporated new and important principles into the code of international law. For, if our country, by its forbearance in the matter of the Trent did much to establish the rights of neutral powers upon the high seas, Mexico, by the prompt execution of the so-called Emperor Maximilian, has done more to establish the Monroe Doctrine than was ever done by Presidential declarations, or by Resolutions of Congress or National Conventions. The essential aid afforded us in our struggle by the persistent adhesion of the Mexican people and their President BENITO JUAREZ, to the cause of their Republic, is felt and acknowledged by every true American. And the sympathy extended to us by Señor ROMERO who, throughout our contest, represented his government near the seat of our own, renders eminently proper and well-timed this manifestation of regard.

I am very respectfully,

Your obedient servant,

HORACE MAYNARD.

Hon. HIRAM BARNEY, Chairman, &c.

Philadelphia, Sept. 28, 1867.

DEAR SIR :

I sincerely regret that public engagements prevent my acceptance of the invitation with which you have honored me to participate in the Dinner to be given to Señor ROMERO, on the 2d inst. It has been my privilege to know Señor ROMERO and to observe his devotion to Republican principles and institutions, and the courage and skill with which he maintained his country's cause, even when, to most men, all seemed lost. It would afford me heartfelt pleasure to meet him before his departure for his home, and publicly express my appreciation of his signal services to the cause of Republicanism.

With thanks for the honor you have done me,

I am, dear sir, very truly yours,

WM. D. KELLY.

Hon. HIRAM BARNEY, Chairman, &c.

[TELEGRAM.]

South Deerfield, Mass., Oct. 2, 1867.

I cannot possibly come, but I congratulate Señor ROMERO with all my heart upon the liberation of his country, and cry amen to every good wish for Mexico.

GEORGE W. CURTIS.

HON. HIRAM BARNEY, Chairman, &c.

Concord, N. H., Sept. 28, 1867.

GENTLEMEN :

Your note inviting me to join with you and the distinguished citizens of New York, whom you represent, at a public Dinner to Señor ROMERO, the honored representative of the Republic of Mexico, on the occasion of his departure for his own country, is received. I assure you, nothing could be more grateful to my feelings than the opportunity of doing honor to one whose genial manners, high personal character and faithful devotion to the liberties and independence of his native land, have justly won for him the gratitude of his own countrymen and the admiration of ours. It is not to be forgotten, on an occasion like the present, that our two sister Republics have just emerged from a common peril at the hands of a common foe. The great rebellion in our country and the Imperial propagandist conspiracy against Mexico, had, if not a common origin, one common object and aim— the overthrow of Republican institutions in America. The adversaries of the United States and of Mexico, were mainly the same, with roles slightly changed. The head of the one conspiracy, was the scarcely less venomous tail of the other ; and both met in the Tuileries. There is an unwritten chapter in the history of both, which will some day see the light. And when it does, it will be seen how narrowly the bolt which fell on Mexico, missed falling on the United States. I state that which I believe, and for which I am not without authority, when I say that the allied British and French naval expedition, which left European waters ostensibly for Vera Cruz, during the pendency of the Trent affair, actually carried contingent orders to proceed to New Orleans, annul the blockade, and proclaim a joint protectorate over all the States bordering on the Gulf of Mexico. How the danger was averted, how the allied fleet went to Vera Cruz, how the

British Government backed out of the Mexican imbroglio, leaving its Imperial ally to proceed alone, and how, after years of heroic endurance and daring, Mexico is at last free from the heel of her invaders, need not here be told. The result has taught the Imperial Master of France a lesson that he will not soon unlearn—that no power is strong enough to enslave a Republican people determined to be free. Thanking you for your invitation, and regretting my inability to be present,

I have the honor to be, gentlemen,

Your obedient servant,

GEORGE G. FOGG.

Hon. Hiram Barney, Chairman, &c.

New York, Sept. 30, 1867.

Sir :

A previous engagement, taking me out of town, prevents my acceptance of the invitation with which your Committee has honored me to a Dinner next Wednesday, in compliment to my friend Señor Romero. For two years past I have had numerous opportunities to witness the vigilance, energy, ability, and self sacrifice which have marked that gentleman's course, as Minister of Mexico, near our Government, and it would have gratified me much to testify in person my appreciation of his great services and eminent worth. Permit me a few words, which, if present, I might have sought occasion to say touching the country which Señor Romero represents. We of Anglo-Saxon blood are wont to decry other races. A recent unhappy event has prompted among us harsh judgment of Mexico; judgment pronounced, I think, without due reflection. Names and titles mislead us. Had a captive captain or lieutenant of the French invading army been shot, in retaliation for similar severity exercised by the invaders, a three-line paragraph, probably, would have been devoted to announcement and comment on the fact ; it would not have caused a ripple on the surface of public opinion. But a Prince, hoister of the black flag, suffers under his own precedent, and a nation is arraigned as

19

barbarous because of the deed. By what rule of ethics is this? Has a man, who happens to be an Emperor's brother, the right to put to death, in cold blood, prisoners charged with nothing which civilization admits to be a crime, and then, because of his rank, to claim exemption from the law he himself set up? Suppose the case our own. Say that in those days when the interest on Pennsylvania bonds remained unpaid, and the Rev. Sydney Smith denounced us a nation of repudiators, we had been but a weak people unable to cope with Great Britain, and that the British Government, not discriminating between State and Federal obligations, had sent an expeditionary army across the Atlantic to enforce payment. Suppose that we had been defeated, the City of Washington taken, our President and his Cabinet driven back into the remote West, a monarchy declared, a prince of the blood royal of England enthroned as King in the White House, our ports seized, our revenues appropriated, a four years desultory war waged to reduce the refractory Republic to order, business suspended, commerce ruined, farms laid waste, tens of thousands of our noblest citizens slain in battle. Suppose that this British Prince had raised the black flag and had shot, by thousands, as bandits, citizens of the United States for the crime of defending the Stars and Stripes. Suppose that our citizens rallying had, by a desperate effort, nearly cleared the country of the British invaders. And suppose, finally, that the self-styled King of the United States, prompted by courage or desperation, had fought to the bitter end and that we had captured him. Let those who denounce Juarez and the Mexican people stand forth and declare whether they would have memorialized our reinstated Government for pardon to the man who had devastated nearly half a continent without even a color of right? Would they have prayed that mercy be shown to him who had shown no mercy to others? Would they have protested against the right of retaliation? Would the American people have permitted the escape of the red-handed usurper merely because he was a queen's son? Thus terribly tempted, should we have followed Christ's precept returning good for evil? If we dare not assert this, let us not contemptuously denounce our neighbors. We are moved to pity for the fate of a brave man, and should lack humanity if the sad recital failed to touch us. But a judge has often sentenced a criminal with trembling voice, and sentence has been confessed to be just, even among the tears of the audience. Posterity may not be able to read, without sorrow, either the story of Eugene Aram, or the history of the misguided and unfortunate Maximilian; but so long as murder is regarded as a crime, it will not acquit either the prince or the scholar.

c

Opposed in principle, to capital punishment, it was my earnest hope, in the interests of civilizations and human progress, that Maximilian's life would be spared. We may justly regret that a people did not rise to the height of such an act of magnanimity. But let us beware how we thank God that we are not as other men. Let us seek to amend, according to principle, a bloody code; but until we shall have succeeded in the effort, let us abstain from judging those who gave way to a temptation which we, similarly situated, would probably have been unable to resist.

I am, sir, your obedient servant,

ROBERT DALE OWEN.

Hon. HIRAM BARNEY, Chairman, &c.

HEADQUARTERS FIRST MILITARY DISTRICT, STATE OF VIRGINIA,
Richmond, Va., Oct. 3, 1867

DEAR SIR :

I have the honor to acknowledge the receipt of an invitation from the Committee of which you were chairman, to a Dinner in compliment to Señor ROMERO, Envoy Extraordinary and Minister Plenipotentiary from Mexico, given in the City of New York on the 2d inst. Sickness prevented your highly esteemed invitation from being brought to my knowledge until this time. Hence the lateness of my reply. Had my health and official duties permitted, it would have afforded me very great pleasure to unite with the citizens of New York in doing honor to Señor ROMERO, for whose personal and official character I have the highest esteem, and to manifest my sincere interest in the welfare of Mexico.

I am, dear sir, yours very truly,

J. M. SCHOFIELD, Major-General.

Hon. HIRAM BARNEY, Chairman, &c.

THE JAY HOMESTEAD, Katonah, Oct. 1, 1867.

MY DEAR SIR:

I pray you to present Señor ROMERO my sincere regrets that I am unable to assist at the Dinner in his honor to be given to-morrow, and at the same time I beg to express my best wishes for himself and his country, to whose service he is about to bring the large experience in statesmanship and diplomacy, acquired during his residence in the United States. The wrongs of Mexico fill a long and dreary page in modern history. With a civilization of her own, dating from the seventh century, and which, at the beginning of the sixteenth, commanded the admiration of her European visitors, she has been made the prey of foreign cupidity and ambition from the invasion of Cortez to that of Louis Napoleon. This fact may go far to explain the origin of those defects in Mexican administration, which Europeans are accustomed to attribute solely to the character of the Mexicans themselves. To this suggestion Europeans might retort—and with justice—that with Texas, California and New Mexico in our possession, it was impudent for an American to broach the topic of Mexican spoliation, and yet Señor ROMERO is undoubtedly right, when he speaks in his letter accepting our invitation, of " the noble sympathies of the American people." The Texan rebellion, and our war with Mexico—its result—were the work of slavery, whose policy of intrigue and conquest was as relentless as that of Spain when ruled by the Inquisition. So also the diplomacy of our government toward Mexico in her recent troubles, as little represented the real sentiments of our loyal citizens. The conquest of Mexico by the French Emperor was, and was intended to be—as Napoleon avowed in his letter to General Foréy—an insult and a menace to the United States, and although, at different stages of its progress, it was acquiesced in, assisted and encouraged by the Department at Washington, the sympathies of our loyal population were always with Mexico and never with her invaders. When in July, 1862, during the active and public preparation for the usurpation of Maximilian, the Department assured Mr. Corwin that it was "very certain that the idea of preparing a throne in Mexico for an Austrian Prince, if ever entertained, was long since abandoned"—when again our Government extended to the French, through the New York Custom House, those facilities for importing into Mexico material of war, which they refused to the Mexicans, calling forth the earnest and dignified protest of your guest ; and when, yet once more, in

October, 1855, Mr. Bigelow, our Minister at Paris, induced M. Drouyn de l'Huys to issue the first order for the return of the French troops by an intimation that the United States would recognize the Empire of Maximilian when they had departed—each and all of these acts of diplomacy—which proved as deplorable in their result as they were vicious in principle—were in direct violation of the sentiments and wishes of the American people, as emphatically declared by our representatives in Congress. Señor Romero, therefore, notwithstanding all that appears doubtful in the acts or the language of our public servants, may safely assure his countrymen, that, as a nation, we sympathize with their resolve to maintain their nationality; and that we shall rejoice at every new indication of the permanence, peace, prosperity and happiness of the Mexican Republic.

I have the honor to be, dear sir,

With great regards, faithfully yours,

JOHN JAY.

Hon. Hiram Barney, Chairman, &c.

State of Rhode Island, Executive Department,
Providence, Oct. 6, 1867.

My Dear Sir :

I found your kind invitation to the Dinner in compliment to Señor Romero on my return home, when it was too late to accept, otherwise would have been glad to have been with you.

With thanks for your kind attention,

I am very truly yours,

A. E. BURNSIDE.

Hon. Hiram Barney, Chairman, &c.

23

St. Louis, Oct. 1, 1867.

SIR :

I have had the honor to receive an invitation from the Committee of which you are chairman, in honor of Mr. ROMERO, Minister of Mexico. If I could, I would accept it, for I would gladly improve any fair occasion to manifest my respect for that worthy gentleman. When I was employed in official duties at Washington, Mr. ROMERO was, all the time, Minister from Mexico; and there were points of mutual sympathy which could not fail to draw us into friendly relations. I believed him an ardent patriot, and devoted to the independence of his country and the freedom of his people ; and I had no reason to doubt but he fully concurred in my own settled belief that popular liberty is impossible, unless it be established and guarded by law. That the military power, so long as it is confined to its legitimate sphere, as the armed servant of the law, to enforce its just authority, is a great protection to the freedom of the people—but when the military power gets above the law, and assumes the sovereignty, there is no instance, in the tide of time, in which it did ever establish and maintain a free, popular government. I am in very low health, confined to my house, now and for many months past ; and, as I cannot appear in person, I venture to send you the following sentiment : " Government by law ; popular liberty protected by law ; and the law equally obligatory upon the few who govern, as upon the many who are governed."

Most respectfully, your obedient servant,

EDWARD BATES.

HON. HIRAM BARNEY, Chairman, &c.

224 West 34th street, New York, Oct. 2, 1867.

MY DEAR SIR :

I regret my inability to attend the reception and Dinner to Señor ROMERO this evening. I have hurt my foot badly, and it is so painful I can scarcely move it. I expected to have had a good time, but I can't.

Sincerely,

SAM'L G. COURTNEY.

HON. HIRAM BARNEY, Chairman, &c.

Columbus, Oct. 2, 1867.

My Dear Sir :

Absence from home prevented my receiving, until this evening, the invitation your committee were kind enough to send me, to attend the Dinner to be given this evening, to Señor Romero. I deeply regret that it will not be in my power to unite with those who will be present, in paying this parting tribute of respect, to one so deserving.

Very truly yours,

N. H. SWAYNE.

Hon. Hiram Barney, Chairman, &c

The honor of

.... company

is requested at a **DINNER** in compliment to

Señor Romero,

Envoy Extraordinary and Minister Plenipotentiary from Mexico.

((AT DELMONICO'S, 14ᵗ ST. & 5ᵗ AVENUE.))

on Wednesday, October 2ⁿᵈ at 6 o'clock.

New York,
September 25ᵗʰ 1867.

Committee

Hiram Barney,
James W. Beekman,
Wm. E. Dodge Jr.,
Theo. Roosevelt,
Henry Clews.

Please reply to
Hiram Barney,
Chairman &c.
New York.

Guests at the Table.

— • • —

Henry Clews, 3d Vice President,

C Romero,	Maj. Gen. Dan'l Butterfield,
Shepard Gandy,	John A. Stewart,
James R. Whiting,	Maj, Gen. Chas. W. Sandford,
F. A, Conkling,	James Robb,
M. H. Grinnell,	Gen. Jas. Grant Wilson,
Prof. Bartlett, West Point,	I. Mariscal,
Wm. Cullen Bryant, President,	Jas. W. Beekman, 1st Vice President,
M. Romero,	A. G. Cattell,
Hiram Barney,	Peter Cooper,
John Russell Young,	E. C. Cowdin,
William E. Dodge, Jr.,	Benj. Halliday,
Maj. Gen. Rufus Ingalls,	Francis Skiddy,
Henry A. Smythe,	Dr. I. N. Navarro,

TABLE.

Theodore Roosevelt, 2d Vice President.

.

Potage.

Hors d'oeuvre.

Timbales.

Entrées.

Rôts.

Entremets.

Sorbets.

Vins.

Entrées.

BANQUET.

The scene on the assembling of the guests was one long to be remembered. The banquetting hall was brilliantly illuminated. The American and Mexican flags were displayed together at either end and suggested the friendly relations of the two countries, while the ornaments of the table, consisting of a temple of liberty and other elaborate designs, seemed to indicate that the United States and Mexico were united in the principles of Republicanism and Independence. Beautiful and rare flowers perfumed the air and charmed the eye, and the Dinner was one of the most splendid entertainments ever given in New York City.

WILLIAM CULLEN BRYANT presided, assisted by JAMES W. BEEKMAN, THEODORE ROOSEVELT and HENRY CLEWS.

The Dinner began at 6 o'clock P. M., and at 9 o'clock Mr. BRYANT requested the attention of the guests and said :

I have a list of toasts which have been handed to me by the Committee of Arrangements, the first of which I will proceed to give out. I hope you will drink it with all the respect that is due to a representative of a Great Republic, and a

D

man who was elected by the great Republican party of the country to take the place of the President in case anything untoward should happen to him. The first toast is

" THE PRESIDENT of the United States." (Applause.)

Mr. BRYANT said:

The next toast relates to the distinguished head of a sister Republic, a person belonging to the old aboriginal stock of the country, through whose instrumentality it seems very likely that Providence designs to restore the ancient prosperity of that country.

" THE PRESIDENT of Mexico." (Three cheers and a tiger.)

Mr. WM. E. DODGE, JR. read the letters received in response to invitations, and the friendly sentiments expressed in them for the guest of the evening and for his country were loudly applauded.

In proposing the third toast Mr. BRYANT said:

GENTLEMEN :—In giving out the third toast of the evening, allow me to introduce it by a few words. We are come together to do honor to a gentleman who for several years past, has represented among us a sister Republic, with an ability worthy of a great cause, and a fortitude and constancy of purpose equal to his ability, (cheers).

There is nothing, my friends, which more surely commands the respect of mankind, and let me say, there are few things that more deserve it than a brave perseverance in a righteous cause, (applause). Of men distinguished by this virtue, history makes up her roll of heroes, and the church her noble army of martyrs. It is most fitting that when such a man has stood firmly by the cause of his country and of liberty, through the years of their greatest adversity and peril, never faltering in his fidelity, never allowing himself to become disheartened by reverses, but resolutely trusting in the final success of the right, until at last he saw it gloriously triumphant—most fitting is it that we should gather around him to congratulate him that his constancy is at last rewarded, that the tyrannical usurpation against which he so steadily protested has been foiled and overthrown, and the liberties which the kings of the earth stood up to destroy has been nobly vindicated. (Cheers.) Such is the man who is now our guest, and such, in brief, is the history of the cause in which he distinguished himself. (Loud cheers.)

We who have all along given that cause our sympathies, and have looked for its triumph as certain to follow the suppression of the Rebellion in our own country, offer him the expression of our sincere rejoicing at the defeat of this attempt to engraft European absolutism upon the institutions of our Continent, and the tribute of our praise for that foresight of his, which beholding the sunshine beyond the tempest, and discerning the sure connection between the cause of Mexico and that of the United States, looked with unwavering confidence for the triumph of both. (Cheers.) The tyranny which the slaveholding class sought to set up in a part of our country has taken its place among the older abortive conspiracies against the welfare of the human race, and the despotism which a great military power of the Old World sought to enthrone in Mexico has been dragged after it in its fall, and now lies with it in the pit. ("Good," and applause.)

While we congratulate our friend on this happy consummation, we should no less congratulate the people of Mexico on having shown, by their obstinate resistance to the imposition of a foreign yoke, and the gallant stand they have made for their independence, that they possess qualities of character for which the world has hitherto given them small credit, and have earned for themselves an honorable name in history. (Cheers.)

There is one act of the Mexican patriots for which they have been greatly maligned, and in defense of which our guest has thought proper at one time to speak. I mean the execution of the pseudo Emperor of Mexico. With regard to the policy of that act I admit that different views may be entertained. I am aware also that there are those who would have had Maximilian spared out of a tender regard for human life, and the feeling which causes a generous nature to shrink from making a victim of an enemy whom we have completely and helplessly in our power. With such I might decline any controversy. But it is not by any such transcendental and unusual standard that the act is to be judged. Its moral quality is to be estimated according to the ideas of justice which prevail throughout civilized countries, and which doom to death him who takes away the life of his fellow man with malice aforethought. (Cheers.)

Maximilian, at a time when his prospects seemed to him brightest, issued a decree to the effect that whosoever was taken in arms, opposing his unprovoked invasion of their country should be tried by a military commission and shot, and this decree was pitilessly executed in numerous instances. The bitter cup which he had forced the innocent to taste has been returned to his own guilty lips. (Loud cheers.) Who that knows this fact can deny that Maximilian deserved death as richly as the ruffian who enters your dwelling at midnight and shoots down the domestics who attempt its defense ? (Cheers.) Let it not be said that he was excusable because he had a principal more guilty than himself, and more deserving of the death of a felon—the Emperor of France. (Cheers.) Napoleon bribed him by the offer of a crown to break into Mexico upon his errand of robbery and and bloodshed He was Napoleon's hired assassin, and I believe that is the utmost that can be said for him. (Applause.)

When, therefore, a peer of Great Britain, and a Prime Minister of the British Empire, rises, in his place, and speaking of the execution of Maximilian, pronounces it a murder, I can find no palliation for so gross an affront to truth, save that it was spoken in shameful ignorance of the facts of history. (Applause.) No, my friends, with all my regard for human life, I find it difficult to answer the arguments of those who urge that so flagrant an offense against the rights of nations as was committed by Maximilian, and such a series of bloody crimes as attended his impious enterprise, deserves something more than that their perpetrator should be dismissed to ease and luxury within the walls of a palace, to be pitied for the rest of his life as a brave and unfortunate man, instead of being shunned as an audacious criminal, but that, on the contrary, he should be subjected to some signal punishment, which should serve as a lesson to future invaders of inoffending Republics, and teach the monarchs of the Old World to respect the liberties of the New. (Long and continued applause.)

But let me return to the subject with which I began, to him whose praise you have heard so largely given in the letters from distinguished men already read. I give the third toast of the evening.

"OUR GUEST, His Excellency Señor MATIAS ROMERO."

This toast was received with the greatest enthusiasm, and when Señor ROMERO rose he was greeted with three cheers. He spoke as follows :

Mr. CHAIRMAN—GENTLEMEN :—It is nearly eight years since I landed in an official capacity on this hospitable shore. Soon afterward I became the representative of my country, or at least of such a portion of it, as believing that they had in the United States a great example to imitate, were eager to give Mexico the same advantages that this country enjoyed, by following the same line of policy.

About that very time, the elements of a gigantic political struggle were maturing, which produced soon afterward the great Civil War of the United States. This terrible shock was felt at once in Mexico, in the shape of an European intervention avowedly for the purpose of overthrowing the Republican institutions existing there. All of you, gentlemen, are quite familiar with what followed here as well as there. It pleased Heaven to crown with success the noble efforts of the patriots and philanthropists, who, while defending in both countries the independence and integrity of their homes, and the institutions of their choice, were also struggling for the advancement of humanity, and the amelioration of the social condition of the masses throughout the world.

I call your attention to this difficult crisis, only to express on this solemn occasion, before this distinguished assembly of representative men, my testimony of the high-toned, enlightened and disinterested sympathy which the cause of Mexico awakened in the hearts of the people of the United States ; a sympathy which, while encouraging the Mexican people in the defense of their outraged rights, made European encroachments more guarded, and thus contributed in a great measure to the final success at which we now all rejoice.

In closing, or at least suspending, temporarily, my official duties at Washington, it behooves me to say, that I carry home a very lively and most pleasant recollection of my long sojourn among you ; that I take also with me the lasting experience of eight years of political agitation, in which very momentous events have taken place ; that faithful to the political creed of the Liberal national party of Mexico, I will do all I can to contribute in establishing there the same political principles I have been taught to appreciate and admire here, and which, in my opinion, are indispensible to the welfare of Mexico ; and it will be my pride as well as my pleasure to be the friend of the United States, so long as they entertain no hostile or unfriendly designs against my own country.

On a former occasion, and in this very place, I availed myself of the opportunity to express what I consider to be a philosophical view, based on facts, of the causes and objects of the civil war in Mexico since the Declaration of its Independence. I do not believe that Nature has made different sets of rules for each people, or for each family of peoples called races. It is, in my opinion, wiser to suppose that Providence controls mankind by the same code of rules, which are equally applicable to the Anglo-Saxon as to the Latin races—to the Indians as to the Africans.

In these modern times, political revolutions seem to have for their object the amelioration of the condition of the masses, by breaking or attempting to break down the old system of the organization of society when this becomes oppressive. Following this theory, it appears to me that in all modern revolutions there have been two sides—the aristocratic side, or the side of the few, who have in the course of time accumulated wealth, power, and influence, often exercised to the disadvantage of the people—and the popular side, or the side of the many, who lose those advantages in proportion as they are monopolized by their opponents. A point is reached where the exactions of the few become intolerable, and then comes a popular uprising; or either, the aristocratic element, foreseeing that this result is to happen, precipitates it, by taking the initiative with a view to forcing the contest, before their enemies are fully organized and prepared. This was, in my opinion, the cause of the English revolution of the 17th century, which culminated in the establishment of the Commonwealth; of the French revolution of the 18th century, which ended in a similar manner; of the last civil war in the United States, and of the civil wars in Mexico and other Spanish American Republics.

Our aristocracy in Mexico has been an ambitious and unscrupulous priesthood, who had wielded for centuries political power, and would rather see their country subjugated by a foreign despot, than under the control of their political opponents, who desire, in good faith, its advancement and prosperity, and its emancipation from religious intolerance, and from opposition to popular and free education. Fortunately for us, the question at home has been of a mere political character, notwithstanding the efforts of the clergy to make it also a religious one.

Our success against the French once achieved, I have very strong and well-grounded reasons to expect that we shall have peace and tranquillity, and that our country will be developed and enjoy fully their attending blessings.

Within a brief period we shall hold our election for the functionaries to be chosen by the people, and we shall then enter again into our constitutional existence, somewhat interrupted by the French intervention. Our policy will then be to enforce our laws, which allow the free exercise of all religions, and give no preference to any; which provide for a perfect separation between Church and State; to establish a system of free schools, which will educate the masses of our people, and make them productive and happy; to encourage the immigration of peaceable and laboring citizens of the United States, which will assist us in developing our resources ; to invite the investment of the surplus capital of the United States in Mexican enterprises, and to look up to this privileged country as to our eldest sister, affording us an example worthy of imitation. When these objects are attained, when both countries stand in the relation of friendly powers, with a common object, and a common destiny, realizing the responsibility they have before the world, as the guardians of Republican institutions, my life-long ambition, and my fondest wishes will have been realized.

The condition of the Mexican people is not fully understood outside of Mexico, and causes very many to distrust their capacity for self-government. It is certainly not so far advanced in civilization as the people of the United States. Education is not so much extended there as it is here ; there is little homogeneousness in the elements of which it is composed ; yet, they are a peaceful, laborious people, well-meaning and docile, and they only need the establishment of free schools and the consolidation of peace, to become one of the best regulated people upon earth. The greater portion of our population has been purposely kept in the most complete ignorance by the Spaniards and the Church party, with a view of controlling them more easily, and when we shall have educated them, we shall double or treble the working energies of the country.

The conduct of the Mexican people during our late war with the French, shows, in my opinion, beyond all doubt, that it possesses very many of the virtues which constitute a free people ; their perseverance under the greatest discouragement, their courage and determination to fight constantly against an enemy vastly superior in resources, their moderation in the hour of success, their well-known endurance, are all facts which speak very clearly in their behalf. I have full confidence in them, and earnestly believe that, if they are not as advanced as it is desirable they should be, they are capable and desirous of improvement.

As to their ability for self-government, I will only say that either Republican institutions are adaptable to mankind, and calculated to promote their welfare and happiness, or they are not. If they are, I see no reason why the Mexican people should be considered unfit for them. If they are not, I could not explain their development in this country.

I think it is a mistaken view of the case to say that because we have had a civil war in Mexico, or rather a social war, which has lasted for many years, it should be concluded that we are incapable of self-government. None can suppose that we have been fighting all that time merely for the pleasure of it. We have had, to be sure, unscrupulous and designing men, who have ostensibly appeared as fighting to gratify their own ambition and self-aggrandizement; but, in fact, they have only been used by one or the other of the contending political parties; and principles have been involved at the bottom of our troubles.

As for the motives which prompted the late Maximilian to go to Mexico—much as I regret to speak of them, since he is now shielded by the sacred asylum of his grave—I, nevertheless, cannot help saying in defence of my own country, that whatever good intentions he may have entertained towards Mexico, if any, they have little to do with the question of his intervention there.

When he was asked to go to Mexico, it is charitable to suppose that he did not understand the true condition of a country so far removed from his own. But the mere fact that he was asked to go by a foreign state, at war with Mexico, and by a few Mexicans who were accomplices in the crime of overthrowing the institutions of their country, by means of a foreign army, it seems to me, ought to have been sufficient to make him very careful before deciding to take part in and increase the political difficulties of Mexico. The inducements held out to him by the French Emperor prevailed at last, and he determined to go under French protection and French auspices, notwithstanding that he never received a single vote from any place in Mexico, not in possession of the French Army of occupation.

The simple case was clearly before him. He may have supposed that if he succeeded in forcing the rule over the Mexican people, he would be the founder of a great European empire in the New World; if he failed, he would return to Europe with the prestige of having attempted to establish one, with the title of Emperor, with a higher position than he ever had before, and a greater probability to succeed his brother as the ruler of the Austrian Empire, or to be the occupant of any vacant throne in that continent.

On leaving Miramar, and before arriving in Mexico, he went to Rome, to secure, as he said, the benediction of the Pope, and what we cannot understand in America, to consult with the Holy See about the temporal government of an American republic. The result was, that notwithstanding that consultation, he not only failed in establishing his rule in Mexico, but that soon after he arrived there he had almost an open rupture with the Pope and the Mexican clergy.

On arriving in Mexico he began to see that his task was more difficult than he had imagined. In the beginning, however, it was but light, as the French Government had taken care to provide him with funds even before he left Europe, making thus of this, another inducement for him to go. When these were exhausted, and the French Emperor—satisfied of the impracticability of his task—made up his mind to withdraw his troops from Mexico, Maximilian thought of returning to Europe as the only alternative left him. I pass over, without comment, the unhappy though not unimportant *role* of the partner of his life. The result of this last and vain effort is well known to all.

Maximilian then determined to carry out his plan of leaving Mexico and sailing from Vera Cruz, where an Austrian war vessel had been in readiness, awaiting to convey him to his home. He came almost by stealth from the City of Mexico to Orizaba, having previously shipped all his baggage and effects, which he took from the country.

On arriving at this latter place, he was overtaken by some of his supporters, who came to persuade him to remain, and who, as they were committed to the Empire, saw in him at least one guaranty of foreign support. They represented to him, as they had done a few years before to the French Emperor, and other European Governments, that they controlled the Mexican people ; that they could give him the men and money necessary to consolidate his rule in Mexico. They enlarged upon the glory he would achieve by accomplishing this result without the aid of the French, and availing themselves of the difficulties which had arisen between him and his supporters, they urged him, by exciting his wounded pride, to make at least another effort to remain, in this instance they succeeded as well as in the former. Their efforts, however, would not have had this result, in my opinion, had they not been supported by the advice of one of Maximilian's most trusted counselors—a Belgian—who accompanied him to Mexico, and who, on writing him a letter from Brussels, on the 17th September, 1866, (the original of which has been in my hands), told him that he ought under no circumstances then to leave Mexico ; that the French desired him to do so, to heap upon him the responsibility of their failure, and that he ought not to gratify them, but, by remaining, place this responsibility where it properly belonged. He advised his master furthermore, to call, after the withdrawal of the French, for a popular election to decide whether the Mexican people desired him or not, as the best means of leaving, without dishonor, a difficult position, and to return to Europe with a prestige.

Maximilian's subsequent action showed that he undertook to carry out to the very letter this advice, given by a man entirely ignorant of the condition of Mexico. He returned to the City of Mexico, after having promised to call for a National Congress to decide whether the people desired the Republic or the Empire under him.

On arriving there he found that the national troops were closing their lines

E

and carrying everything before them, and, supposing that he could arrest these advances by taking to the interior all the available forces accumulated in the City of Mexico, he marched to Queretaro. It would be unnecessary to say what happened there. Through the want of military ability he allowed our troops to concentrate upon and besiege Queretaro, until he was finally overcome. From the tenor of his communications while he was surrounded at Queretaro, it appears very clearly that he never realized the difficulties of his position, and much less the disastrous end of the campaign ; and his letters to President JUAREZ since he was captured, showed not less plainly that, until then, he had never dreamed of the sad fate which, by invading a harmless and innocent people in their American mountain homes he had provoked and deserved.

But Maximilian, although a Grand Duke and heir of empire in Austria, was nothing of a Cæsar, and only a French automaton in the revolutionary drama of my country. Let this unhappy fate be accepted in extenuation of his crime, in consenting to be the automaton of the ambition of the French Cæsar in the revolution of Mexico.

Mexico can hereafter have no fears, for her safety against foreign invasion is assured ; no revenges will follow the revolution which her enemies inaugurated, and which has resulted in their own overthrow and ruin.

In concluding these remarks, I fear I have already intruded too long upon your patience (cries of " No, no.") I must say that I believe the Mexican Government is preparing several documents to be given to the world, in which its position and the relations of Maximilian towards Mexico will be fully explained. I am certain when these documents see the light, that all who doubted the correctness and propriety of the policy adopted by the Mexican Government, will be inclined to change their minds. I cannot resume my seat without again thanking the gentlemen present this evening for their kindness and courtesy in tending to me this demonstration. I shall always remember it as one of the most pleasant evenings, and one of the most pleasing events that has taken place in my life.

Senor ROMERO's speech was loudly applauded throughout.

Mr. BRYANT read the next toast:

" MEXICO, our sister Republic, may she ever remain, as the constancy she has so recently shown in defending her national liberties proves her worthy to remain, independent and free." (Cheers.)

and called upon Señor I. Mariscal, acting Minister of Mexico during the absence of Señor Romero, to respond.

Señor Mariscal said:

Gentlemen—I would never speak quite unprepared and in a language not my own, before an assembly like this, for I naturally feel embarrassed before such a presentation of the high sense, the talent, the poetry, and the eloquence of the country, but since I cannot properly omit saying something, after the invitation of our venerable Chairman, I will confine myself to a few words.

More than three years ago several persons of the *elite* of New York tendered to Mr. Romero a demonstration just as significant as this. It was an encouragement offered to a struggling Republic in her darkest hour, and her representative at the beginning of his arduous task, and I can assure you, that in unison with other friendly demonstrations from this great people, it reëchoed in the hearts of all true Mexicans. (Cheers.) This token of yours, so well worded in the toast you have just drunk, seems to me to have a peculiar meaning. It is not only a congratulation offered to the triumphant Mexican Republic itself, but to a certain extent an approval of the conduct of her government. This approval of yours, gentlemen, has great political weight, for it comes from real American notables, from the real aristocracy of the country—the only one consistent with Democratic institutions, the aristocracy of industry, of talent, of virtue, in other words, the aristocracy of personal merit. (Applause.) Its significancy will be well understood and appreciated in Mexico.

Our people are now engaged in the work of reconstruction, and it will encourage them to follow in the path of this model Republic, while trying to develope those great principles of Republicanism taught by you and for which they have so freely and so bravely shed their blood. (Loud cheers.) Gentlemen, when the intelligence of this demonstration reaches Mexico, all my fellow citizens will be most thankful. At this moment I feel more than I can express. (Applause.)

The fifth toast was read as follows:

" Free Churches and Free Schools, the true guarantees of individual and natural happiness, and the aim of Mexican patriots."

Mr. BRYANT said that he felt obliged to call upon a gentle-man not unacquainted with evangelical and educational affairs, and who had interested himself much in their progress in this country, Mr. JAMES W. BEEKMAN. (Applause.)

Mr. BEEKMAN said:

Mr. PRESIDENT—I do not know that the number five is considered a particularly good number, but I know that the fifth desk in the New York Senate procured me the present distinction. It was there, sir, that I learned to value free schools, and when in response to your command I rise to reply to a toast which it was expected another would respond to, I must begin by saying that to the children of the free schools in Mexico, the Lancasterian school established by General TORNEL, forty years ago, we owe all that has been done in Mexico. (Cheers.) The Liberal party in Mexico is composed of the men and women who have been trained in those schools, and who there learned that it is possible to worship God and serve the state in more ways than one only, which glorious lesson, I take it, lies at the foundation of our prosperity, as it lies at the root of a certain tree of liberty planted in a very moist soil on the other side of the water many centuries ago. (Cheers.) I have the honor to spring from. that tree, and in my fatherland I know very well that a paper bull was fulmi-nated many years ago which remains infallible and unrevoked, by which my fore-fathers and myself are consigned to perdition for free schools, and therefore I hail with joy the efforts made in Mexico in their behalf as the harbinger of better days, as the standard, full high advanced, of free and unforced conscience, of liberty, and the union of education and religion, one and inseparable, now and forever. (Cheers.)

The sixth toast was read:

"REPUBLICAN GOVERNMENT on the American continent the common cause of every community in the Western hemisphere." (Hearty cheers.)

Mr. F. A. CONKLING responded:

Mr PRESIDENT AND GENTLEMEN—Within the last six years the couter-minous Republics of the United States and Mexico have incontestably demonstrated to the world the fidelity, I had almost said the morality of Republican institutions in the Western hemisphere. They have proved that no combination of circumstances can be so desperate that the principle of government by the people for the people, will not in the end triumphantly reässert its supremacy. (Cheers.) In our own country we have seen twelve millions of people in arms to overthrow the government, inhabiting a territory imperial in its extent, of unquestionable fertility, intersected by a mighty mountain range and by the greatest river system of the world, abounding in almost inaccessible fastnesses and everglades, with a proud and haughty dominant race, impelled by the prospect of almost oriental indulgences and splendors—we have seen all this, sir, and yet to-day we see the United States more powerful than ever before ; her flag floating triumphantly over every foot of her original territory, while the sun rises upon no master and sets upon no slave, and stretching her dominions a thousand miles further towards the frozen regions of the North. (Applause.)

In the midst of our great struggle an arrogant and rapacious monarchy of the Old World cast her evil eye upon our sister Republic of Mexico, and she selected as her instrument a prince of the oldest royal house in all Europe   That prince justly sleeps to-night in a tyrant and usurper's grave. (Cheers.)   Juarez all the time was flying from state to state with the government, until finally the usurper proclaimed that constitutional liberty had forever fled the country ; but Juarez, whether accompanied by ten thousand or only ten followers, representing the great principle of Republican liberty was stronger than all the myrmidons of the tyrant, and to-day he stands in the halls of the Montezumas reaping the reward of faithfulness to liberty and his country. (Cheers.) Although the cause of Mexico and the United States was one, it was ordained by Providence that each should fight its battles alone, and it is fitting to remark here, that the honored representative of the Mexican Government, near the United States, at all times, hoping almost against hope, continued his efforts with a sad constancy that could not be denied, until finally his faith in justice and in God conquered victory, (cheers,) and when hereafter the roll of the illustrious patriots and benefactors shall be called, the name of Matias Romero shall stand high among them all, (Cheers.) In conclusion, Mr. President, permit to give you :

The United States and Mexico, twin bulwarks of Republican freedom. They will take care that no European power shall hereafter interfere with the institutions of those who dwell on this side of the Atlantic. (Cheers.)

The seventh toast was drank:

" The moral to be deduced from recent events in Mexico—an admonition to the great powers of Europe that they cannot intermeddle with the institutions of those who dwell on this side of the Atlantic. (Applause.)

THE PRESIDENT called upon Major Gen. SANDFORD to respond to this toast.

Gen. SANDFORD said :

Mr. PRESIDENT :—I did not expect to be called upon to-night when there are so many eloquent friends around me, but there is certainly no more important sentiment to the people of this entire Continent, than the one which you have just uttered.   Europe has ridiculed the idea embodied in what is called the Monroe Doctrine, but of its wisdom, of its soundness, of its importance not merely to the United States, but to this entire Continent, there can be no doubt.   There is no principle which, to-day, Americans should so strongly advocate, for the world at large can no longer ridicule it.   The time has come when the Monroe Doctrine may be proclaimed in stentorian tones, and can be enforced with an energy which Europe must shrink back from.   (Applause.)

The time has come when the associated Republics of the Western World may set at defiance the whole association of despots in Europe. (Cheers.)   The power which this Republic developed during the late Civil War, has created a feeling of astonishment and I may say alarm among the European nations, and I venture to predict that from this time forward, there will be no more ridicule of the Monroe Doctrine, or intermeddling on the part of foreign despots with the liberties of associated America. (Cheers.)

We have at length become one of the powers of the earth.   The energy, the skill and the science exhibited by our nation during the late war, has awakened a new era among the naval and military men of Europe. They no longer regard American inventions with contempt, they no longer talk of " American notions," they know and they fear American skill and American prowess, and we need no longer be afraid of an intervention with American Republics. (Cheers.)

Mr. BRYANT said :

There is a gentleman here, the accomplished commercial representative of Mexico in this city, Dr. NAVARRO, from whom we should like to hear a word or two in relation to the affairs of his country, and in partial response perhaps to the toast that has already been given.

Dr. NAVARRO was greeted with applause. He said :

Mr. CHAIRMAN and GENTLEMEN, being entirely unprepared you will allow me to make only a few remarks. Three and a half years ago, I had the honor of being invited by some of you to this very place, where you met to express your sympathy for the Mexican Republic, then struggling for her life with one of the most powerful European monarchies. Your own country at that time was also shaken by a gigantic Civil War, fomented and applauded by the enemies of Republican institutions all over the world. (Applause.) On that occasion the situation of the two Republics was identical and so were our convictions. No one of those present doubted for a moment that the glorious cause of the Union would achieve a most complete and splendid triumph, or that the Republic of Mexico would spring up, as it were, from her own ashes, and be forever free and independent. (Cheers.) Our mutual wishes and conviction, thanks to heaven, have been fulfilled. Your magnificent country is and shall be one (" Bravo," and applause), and mine, though weakened and almost exhausted, after so long and bloody a strife, waves to the wind, on the snowy summit of her colossal mountains, the dear old flag, where our nation can read the magical words, " Republic" and " Independence."

Under such pleasing circumstances as the present, I feel obliged as a Mexican to make manifest to you, and through you to all your fellow citizens, my heartfelt gratitude for the unfaltering and efficient moral support given to our cause by both the public officials and citizens of this great Republic, (cheers,) and for that generous hospitality which, lavished upon every one of us in our bitterest hours, made us forget we were exiles, and hail your beautiful country as our second home. (Cheers.)

My most fervent wishes are for the uninterrupted prosperity and welfare of the United States, for the unity of sentiment among all its inhabitants, and for the everlasting existence of this impregnable bulwark of human liberty. (Cheers.)

Mr. BRYANT said :

I see one of the distinguished commanders of our forces in the late Rebellion present, General BUTTERFIELD, who, I am told will not be unwilling to say a word or two for the edification of the company. I therefore call upon Gen. BUTTERFIELD. (Applause.)

Gen. BUTTERFIELD said :

Mr. PRESIDENT AND GENTLEMEN, I confess that by the remarks of your worthy and venerable Presiding Officer, my flank is completely turned. (Laughter and applause.) It was personally understood when I came here this evening, with the gentlemen who have had charge of this elegant entertainment, that I should not be called upon to speak.

Mr. BRYANT :—I was not aware of that. It was not my fault.

Gen. BUTTERFIELD :—I have been a quiet listener to the sentiments that have been expressed here this evening, and I should not have been willing to respond to the call of your President, had not the remarks I have listened to prompted me to one theme, the philosophical deduction of all that has passed here, and that is that we see that the people of Mexico, without our aid, other than our moral sympathy, have achieved their own freedom and their own independence. It teaches us that governments rest with the people, that a people unworthy of their own independence cannot gain it, (applause,) and I give you as my sentiment :

The heart and the intellect of a free and educated people the perfect basis of a just Government. (Cheers.)

HON. JAS. R. WHITING was called upon for a speech.

Mr. WHITING said :

MEXICO, GOD BLESS HER! when she rises from the wounds and bruises imposed upon her, let her remember that in the year 1862, her distinguished representative, who is now our guest, stood firm as adamant on the rock of liberty, (applause,) his hopes in the future being beautifully expressed in the language of our poet, who presides for us on this occasion:

> " Truth crushed to earth will rise again,
> The eternal years of God are hers;
> But error, wounded, writhes in pain,
> And dies amid her worshippers."

(" Good" and cheers).

The truth of Mexico was centred in her liberty, and although crushed to earth, she has risen again, realizing the promise of the poet. (Applause.) She has lifted her head among the nations of the earth, and to-day she stands before us giving evidence to the world that divinity doth not hedge a king. (Loud cheers.) I do not stand here to justify the policy, but as an American citizen, I justify the principle which led to the tragical result, that any man of ordinary common sense must have foreseen, and he who could not see it ought to die. (Cheers.) I congratulate you, Señor Romero, upon the success of your country. I have known you since 1862, and I have endeavored to stand shoulder to shoulder by you in the efforts you have made in its behalf.

Mr. Romero:—You have, sir.

Mr. Whiting—And when you return to the Palace of the Montezumas, I beg you to make my most profound respects to Señor Juarez, who will live hereafter upon the page of history as a hero devoted to the establishment of civil and religious liberty within the limits of the State of Mexico. (Applause.) I have witnessed, sir, the assiduity and unflagging zeal which you have displayed in the cause of your country. I have known your hopes, your fears and your anxieties, and throughout your many trials you have had my warmest sympathy. When you return home, may God speed you there, may the breezes of prosperity waft you upon the ocean, and may your people extend to you the hearty welcome you so well deserve. I have no doubt from my personal intercourse with you, that you can lay your hand upon your breast, and say to President Juarez, "Sir, I return to you the talents that you committed to my care, there they are with all the usury that I have been able to add to them." Your countrymen have established a written fundamental Constitution and have broken the shackles of slavery, and while I admire *their* heroism and *their* devotion to liberty, I also rejoice as a citizen of this great Republic, that as regards slavery, *our* Constitution now stands transcendantly above that which we have heretofore worshipped, and that now after a long struggle—in which we have paid the penalty—humanity is disenthralled.

If my blood ever tingled in my veins as an American citizen, it was when I received a letter from the Collector of the port of Quebec, telling me in the English language, and underscoring what he wrote, that "Canada is free," while we were struggling for civil and personal liberty in my own country. Yes, sir, that was his message to me when I was obliged to ask him whether he would not allow me to furnish a little aid to Mexico when that privilege was refused me by my own country. Our citizens have cause to hang their heads with shame when they reflect upon the position occupied by our Government towards Mexico in the hour of her greatest danger. A few words at that time spoken by our Secretary of State to impudent France, to the effect that the United States regarded the intervention of Napoleon in the affairs of Mexico with disapprobation, would have saved your people thousands of lives and millions of money, and would also have been of incalculable benefit to ourselves in the war we were then waging, by showing to the world that we had faith in God, faith in the justice of our cause, and strength and courage to uphold it. (Applause.)

Much has been said against the policy of your Government, but nothing can be said against its justice. The treatment of Maximilian was a matter exclusively your own, he violated your laws and he suffered under your laws. Those here who think that he ought to have been treated with charity, clemency and mercy, would, no doubt, if they had lived in Mexico, have insisted upon his execution. It is an easy thing to indulge a forgiving disposition when you are not the person who suffers the wrong. From our stand point it may seem that Maximilian should have been treated with clemency, charity and mercy, but in Mexico justice and even their existence as an independent state demanded his execution. (Cheers.) Besides, he richly deserved his punishment, and is no more entitled to our sympathy than the worst criminal who suffers for his crimes.

What did he do? "Tell it not in Gath, proclaim it not in the streets of Askalon." He published a proclamation directing the execution of every man, within twenty four hours after he should be found in arms against this imperial edict, and by his order some of the noblest blood of Mexico was spilled for no other offense than devotion to country.

The fate of Maximilian is a lesson and a warning to the crowned heads of Europe to avoid hereafter any interference in the affairs of this hemisphere. I have no doubt that President JUAREZ, so far as his own feelings were concerned, inclined to the side of mercy and wished to save Maximilian, but he owed a duty to his country, and like Washington during the war of the Revolution, when the fate of Major André was in his hands, he was obliged to make the sacrifice to save his people. (Cheers.)

In conclusion, I say, God speed your President, God speed your country, God speed you, and may all the blessings of heaven be showered upon your head from this time forever and ever. (Cheers.)

Mr. Romero said :

I think I owe it to Judge Whiting to make a statement of facts here which are very honorable to him, and although I am afraid I shall offend his modesty, I cannot refrain from referring to them. It was my fortune to know Judge Whiting at a time when circumstances were very unfavorable to Mexico, in the Summer of 1862, when it was very difficult, almost impossible, as it proved afterwards, to export to my country any arms or munitions of war, of which we were in great need. Although the laws of the United States permitted the exportation of all sorts of articles and goods, some way was found to prevent the exportation of such things as we needed, and I think it is but simple justice to Judge Whiting to say, that he exerted himself in every possible way to have the restriction removed. He went to Washington several times, and used his influence with the Departments there, and also applied to the Collector of the port here, to enable us to take out arms which were needed in Mexico, and which he thought we had a perfect right to do. This is a fact known to very few persons outside of the official circles at Washington and the Collector at this port, who was then our good friend Mr. Barney ; but I can assure the Judge that I have put all the facts on record and have filed all the papers, including the able arguments submitted by him to the Treasury Department and to the Collector of the port of New York, and I hope at some future time to do justice to his efforts by bringing them all to light. I am quite satisfied that the Mexican people and the public at large will always honor him for his efforts in support of the noble cause with which he has been identified all his life, and for which, in this instance, he did all that it was in his power to do. (Applause.)

Mr. Beekman said :

We have here a gentleman who is familiar with Mexico, who has served on the border, and who can say some words worth hearing. I allude to Gen. James Grant Wilson. (Applause.)

Gen. WILSON said :

I had the honor of being a volunteer in the late war, and I will now volunteer a word, a single word. After what has been said in regard to Mexico by the eloquent gentlemen who have preceded me, I do not know that I can add anything, but I desire the gentlemen here present to join with me in drinking the health of our honored Chairman, one whose name and fame will be always prized, " with earth's and sea's rich gems, with April's first-born flowers, and all things rare." (Cheers.)

Mr. BRYANT said :

I can only thank the gentleman who has been so kind as to offer the toast, and the company for the great good nature they have shown in accepting it. and accompanying it with applause. (Cheers.)

This concluded the entertainment, and the company separated, after taking an affectionate leave of their distinguished Guest.